This is a fictionalised biography describing some of the key moments (so far!) in the career of Jude Bellingham.
Some of the events described in this book are based upon the author's imagination and are probably not entirely accurate representations of what actually happened.

Tales from the Pitch
Jude Bellingham
by Matt Carver

Published by Raven Books
An imprint of Ransom Publishing Ltd.
Unit 7, Brocklands Farm, West Meon, Hampshire GU32 1JN, UK
www.ransom.co.uk

ISBN   978 180047 806 0
First published in 2024
Reprinted 2024

Copyright © 2024 Ransom Publishing Ltd.
Text copyright © 2024 Ransom Publishing Ltd.
Cover illustration by Ben Farr © 2024 Ben Farr

A CIP catalogue record of this book is available from the British Library.

All rights reserved. No part of this publication may be reproduced, stored in a retrieval system, or transmitted, in any form or by any means, electronic, mechanical, photocopying, recording or otherwise, without the prior permission of the publishers.

The right of Ben Farr to be identified as the illustrator of this Work has been asserted by him in accordance with sections 77 and 78 of the Copyright, Design and Patents Act 1988.

TALES FROM THE PITCH

JUDE BELLINGHAM

MATT CARVER

RAVEN

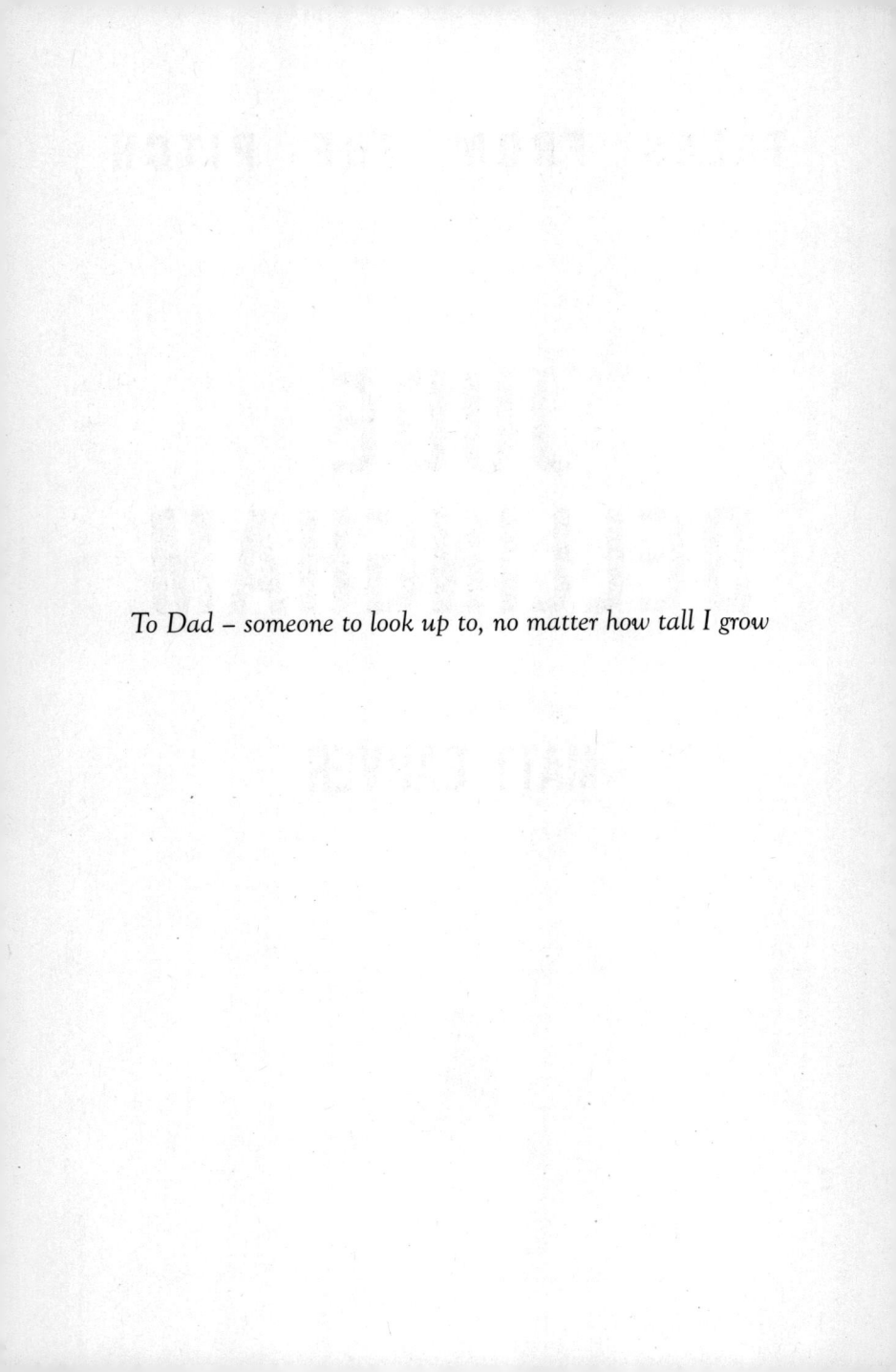

To Dad – someone to look up to, no matter how tall I grow

CONTENTS

		Page
1	No Stage Too Big	7
2	Catching the Bug	15
3	Once a Blue	19
4	Schoolboy Football	24
5	Blues Debut	31
6	Cold Night Against Stoke	37
7	Always a Blue	43
8	Like a Duck to Water	49
9	The First of Many	54
10	Trophy Cabinet	59
11	Under the Arches	64
12	The Bridesmaid	70
13	Brace Yourself	77
14	On the World Stage	82
15	One Day	87
16	So Close	93
17	The Next Galáctico	99
18	Hey Jude	103
19	Golden Boy	108
20	Hala Madrid	112

1
NO STAGE TOO BIG

April 2021, Westfalenstadion, Dortmund, Germany
Champions League Quarter-Final, Dortmund v Man City

"No. No way," exclaimed Pep Guardiola, shaking his head in disbelief. "You're telling me that Jude Bellingham is still only seventeen?"

Just two hours earlier, Jude Bellingham had walked out for the biggest game so far in his young career. He was in his first season with the huge German club, Borussia Dortmund, and this season they had made it to the Champions League quarter-final. The first leg, at the Etihad Stadium the previous week, had finished 2-1 to Man City, and Jude had been denied a goal by a marginal refereeing decision.

So today, for the second leg, at the Westfalenstadion, Jude was striding onto the pitch alongside Dortmund's lethal Norwegian striker, Erling Haaland.

Both players knew what they had to do. Haaland had already scored 10 goals in the Champions League this season, and he was always keen to remind Jude of that.

"Going to actually score today then, Jude, rather than just foul the keeper?" Erling laughed. Jude hadn't yet scored in the Champions League, despite ten appearances in the competition.

"Just make sure you score enough to win us the game!" Jude replied with a grin. He was desperate to win the tie and reach the semi-finals – getting a goal would just be a bonus.

Dortmund had scored a valuable away goal in the first leg, so a 1-0 win today would be enough to put them through to the next stage.

Jude looked across the pitch at the Man City players as

they were going through their stretches, ahead of kick-off. He could see a world-class player in every position. Kevin De Bruyne, the technical master, was standing at the centre of attack. To his left was Phil Foden, Jude's England team-mate. This wasn't going to be an easy task.

The first few minutes were cagey, as both teams eased into the match.

At home games, Dortmund were ordinarily cheered on by around 80,000 roaring fans, which made the players feel as if they had an extra man on the pitch.

But today it was eerily quiet. The COVID-19 pandemic restrictions meant that the stands that Jude usually looked up to for motivation were completely empty. Today, he would have to find his own inspiration.

After 15 minutes, Dortmund's German defensive midfielder, Emre Can, received the ball in space. Looking up, he launched a searching ball forward for Erling Haaland to chase.

Erling held the ball up, before playing it into the path of Mahmoud Dahoud, whose shot on goal was blocked by a Man City defender. Suddenly, the ball was loose on the edge of the penalty area.

Jude was the quickest to react, picking it up on his left foot, before quickly swivelling onto his right. He didn't even need to look to know where the goal was. Instinctively, he opened his body and fired the ball into the top corner of the goal, past the despairing dive of the City keeper.

"GOAL!" cried Jude, running away to the corner of the pitch to celebrate.

He was quickly mobbed by his team-mates, and together they cheered into the lens of a nearby TV camera.

Jude wanted the absent fans to be able to share the moment, and he knew his parents and brother would be watching as well.

"Not bad, Jude, not bad at all!" Haaland grinned. "I reckon you've been watching me and taking notes."

Jude enjoyed the joke, feeling relieved that he'd finally scored his first Champions League goal.

Dortmund now had their precious 1-0 lead and were winning the tie. All they had to do was survive the next 75 minutes without conceding – against one of the best teams in the world.

Just 10 minutes later, Dortmund had their first scare.

De Bruyne stole the ball on the edge of the Dortmund

area, before crashing a first-time shot against the crossbar and away.

Five minutes later, Riyad Mahrez won the ball in a deep area for Man City, before playing a long diagonal ball to Phil Foden. Foden took the ball down with a perfect first touch, then hooked it back across the face of the Dortmund goal.

Mahrez was following up and took one touch to control the ball, before stroking it past the Dortmund keeper. Scrambling back, Jude stretched out his left leg and was just able to divert the ball behind for a corner.

That had been very close. The pressure on Dortmund was building.

"Focus, boys! Focus. We need to be better than this!" Jude yelled, trying to rally his team-mates. Despite his young age, he was a leader in this team – it just came naturally to him.

Man City's threat continued to mount and, minutes later, De Bruyne whipped in a dangerous corner. Oleksandr Zinchenko met the ball, sending a threatening header towards goal. But the Dortmund keeper, Marwin Hitz, stood firm and plucked the ball out of the sky.

Dortmund spent the rest of the first half defending for their lives, so the referee's half-time whistle came as a relief to the home team.

Jude was breathing heavily as he trudged into the dressing room at half-time. He felt as if he'd spent the entire first half chasing hard. For the second half, Dortmund needed to find a way to get back on the front foot. After all, they still had their 1-0 lead – they were already half-way to the semi-final.

Jude waited until his manager, Edin Terzić, had talked to the team, then stood up and motioned for the players to be quiet.

"This is our chance, boys," Jude began, hoping to fire up his team-mates. "We have the lead – all we have to do is keep a clean sheet and we'll be into the Champions League semi-final. We're here because we're good enough. Now let's go back out and show it!"

Even though many of the players were a decade older than Jude, they all cheered in response.

Man City came out for the second half with renewed energy and immediately wrestled control of possession from Dortmund.

The home team could only hold their lead for six minutes.

Foden swung in a cross from the left flank and, as Emre Can stooped to head the ball away, it struck his outstretched arm. In the empty stadium, the referee's whistle sounded incredibly loud. Penalty to Man City.

Riyad Mahrez stepped up confidently and smashed the ball home. It was 1-1. Man City had their own away goal.

Now Dortmund needed to score again just to make it to extra-time – and they needed two goals to win.

The Dortmund players rallied, knowing that it was now or never. If they let Man City score again, it would surely mean the end of their Champions League campaign.

The Dortmund pressure started to pay off and they won themselves a free kick in a threatening area. Mats Hummels, the powerful Dortmund centre-back, met the free kick with a strong header that flew narrowly over the bar.

Even though Dortmund kept on fighting, Man City were a massively experienced team. They'd been in this position countless times before and they weren't going to give up their lead at this stage. The City players kept streaming forward in attack, not giving Dortmund a chance to get back in the game.

With just 15 minutes remaining, Bernardo Silva played a short corner to Foden on the edge of the Dortmund box. Foden took one touch, before rifling an unstoppable shot into the Dortmund goal.

It was 2-1 to Man City – game over. Even if Dortmund scored twice now, they would still be losing on away goals.

The referee's final whistle brought Jude's first season in the Champions League to an end. He knew he'd played well, but he was bitterly disappointed not to have gone further in the competition.

After the teams had left the pitch, Pep Guardiola, the legendary manager of Man City, was interviewed by the awaiting journalists.

One of the first questions he was asked was, "Can you believe that Jude Bellingham is *that* good, at only 17 years old?"

2
CATCHING THE BUG

August 2009, Stourbridge, West Midlands, England

Jude wandered away from the training session and sat down in the field. He started to pick aimlessly at the grass, bored and wishing he was back at home.

A ladybird landed on his hand and he watched it walk along the back of his finger, until it spread its wings and flew away.

"Jude, come and get stuck in!" called Mark

Bellingham, who was standing with the other children. Jude could hear their shouts as they played a small match.

"I'm alright, Dad. I don't want to play," Jude replied, gazing at the grass that pressed against his boots.

"But you were so good in the warm-up. None of the others could catch you in the 'cat and mouse'," his dad said encouragingly, as he made his way over to Jude.

Sensing that he wasn't persuading his son, Mark switched to a different tack.

"Jobe is going to join in today. Do you think he'll be better than his big brother?" Mark asked, knowing that this would get a rise from Jude. Even though they were still very young, the brothers were extremely competitive.

Without waiting for a response from Jude, Mark walked back over to the training session and asked Jude's younger brother, Jobe, to join in.

Jobe was good for his age – *very* good. After a few minutes, he ran onto a pass and kicked the ball as hard as he could, sending it flying past the youngster in goal.

"Goal!" cried Mark, lifting Jobe up in celebration.

Then Mark turned towards the touchline and saw

that, as he'd expected, Jude had quietly come back over to watch the game. Without saying anything, Mark handed a bib to Jude and gestured that he should join the team playing against Jobe.

Jude ran onto the pitch and immediately the ball was passed to him. He strode forward, brushing off a challenge from one of the children on the opposing team.

Then, seeing Jobe up ahead, Jude burst past him and fired a shot on goal, beating the keeper.

"Anything you can do, I can do better," Jude called playfully to Jobe. Mark just smiled.

For the rest of the game, Jude was unstoppable. He was only six years old, but he was quicker and better on the ball than any of the other children.

In fact, Jude was enjoying himself immensely, lapping up the praise that was offered each time he scored a goal or made a tackle.

When they got home after training, Denise Bellingham, Jude's mum, pulled Mark aside.

"How did they get on?" she asked quietly. "If Jude still doesn't want to play, you'd better stop taking him."

"Mum, I *loved* it," grinned Jude, who'd overheard his mum's question. "And I did even better than Jobe," he added proudly.

The next day, the Bellingham family went to watch Mark play in a match for the local team. Jude usually dreaded these Sunday mornings, spent standing in the cold pretending to enjoy watching his father playing football.

But this time, Jude couldn't take his eyes off the game.

His dad scored a hat-trick, and each time he scored he ran over to celebrate the goal with his sons.

For the first time, Jude noticed the excitement in the crowd every time the ball was near the goal – and he could feel that excitement himself too.

Something had clicked in Jude's mind. Now, there was nothing he wanted more than to be on that pitch, scoring the goals himself.

3
ONCE A BLUE

August 2010, Stourbridge, West Midlands, England

Jude was good. He was far too good for his age group – and he was too good even for the age group above his.

He'd been going to training for a year now, and every Saturday morning he would win the warm-up games, the tag matches *and* the races.

Then, whichever team he was on would win all the drills and matches they'd play that day.

Having Jude on your team might be a guarantee that you'd never lose, but Mark was starting to worry. He was afraid that Jude would get bored again and would lose interest in football. It was all just too easy for him.

"Jude, I've got something to tell you," Mark said, beckoning his son over at the end of another successful training session.

"You're too young to play for Stourbridge in proper matches," Mark continued. "Or at least, you *were*. But I've created a new team for your age group. Now you'll be able to test yourself in proper matches."

Beaming, Jude looked up at his dad.

"Will you be there too, Dad?" he asked.

"Of course, Jude. I'll be the manager. But I won't go easy on you, just because I'm your dad," he laughed. "You know that."

"It's good you'll be there. Then you'll get to watch me win," Jude said, seriously.

And win he did. The next weekend, Stourbridge Juniors kicked off the season, and Jude proudly lined up wearing a red and white striped kit which hung down to his thighs.

For Jude, playing for Stourbridge Juniors was really no different from training. Just moments into their first game, Jude demanded the ball, and was passed it on the right wing. Even on these smaller pitches, designed for the under-eights, he could find space.

Jude chopped inside onto his left foot, sending his marker in the wrong direction. Then he drifted forward, skipping past another challenge with ease. Now he was through on goal.

Calmly he flicked the ball past the keeper and into the net. Then, with barely any celebration, he just ran back to his half and waited for the restart.

It carried on like this for the next few months, with Jude totally dominating play.

Mark's old worries that Jude would get bored began to creep back in.

"Maybe he just needs to play against better teams," Denise suggested.

"There aren't any better teams at our level," said Mark. "This is it."

"What about Birmingham?" asked Denise. "You know he wants to play for them."

Birmingham City were one of the biggest clubs in the area, along with their rivals, Aston Villa.

"Yeah – them and England!" Mark chuckled. "But maybe you're right, Denise. Birmingham would definitely be a serious step up – he'd be playing in a Premier League team's academy."

At Stourbridge Juniors' next game, all appeared normal. Jude ran the show as usual, scoring twice and winning 'man of the match'.

And, as usual, Mark coached him from the touchline, offering snippets of advice here and there.

Except that this time, when Jude was leaving with his dad after the match, a man approached them both.

"Hello, Mark. Thanks for inviting me down. Quite a player you've got yourself there," said Lyndon Tomlinson.

"Jude – this is Lyndon. He's a scout for the Birmingham City academy," said Mark.

"Did you see me play? And did you see my second goal?" Jude asked excitedly.

"Of course I did. I wouldn't be much of a scout if I didn't watch the game!" Lyndon grinned.

"Good. I want to be a professional footballer and play for Birmingham," Jude replied firmly.

Lyndon smiled, surprised by Jude's determination. "Hopefully we can help you with that, young man."

A few days later, Jude was standing on the touchline at St. Andrew's, Birmingham City's stadium. He couldn't stop smiling.

"Over here!" called the photographer. Jude and Denise looked at the camera, and Jude pretended to sign a piece of paper that was resting on a table in front of him.

"Welcome to Birmingham City, Jude."

4
SCHOOLBOY FOOTBALL

May 2017, Bodymoor Heath, West Midlands, England

"Do you feel like a traitor, playing here?" Odin Bailey asked, as he and Jude climbed down the steps of the school bus.

"Nah. We'll just treat it like an away derby for Birmingham – you know, beating Villa in their own back yard," Jude replied.

Odin and Jude played together in the Birmingham

City academy and, although Odin was a few years older, they were both in the same school team.

As the pair wandered into the dressing room at Aston Villa's training ground, they saw the rest of their team staring at the facilities around them, impressed by the immaculate pitches and the professional environment.

This was all something Jude had got used to by now.

"Come on in, boys." Their PE teacher, who also acted as the football team's coach, was calling them over. "You've done well to get this far. Reaching the semi-finals of a national cup is a big achievement in itself," he said, as he began what he hoped would be an inspirational team talk.

"But with a win today, we'll be back here next week for the final – with the chance to bring some silverware to the Priory School and to put your names in the school history books."

The players cheered in response, encouraged by their teacher's words, but Jude just smiled.

He wasn't motivated by school football trophies. He was doing well in the Birmingham City academy and felt that he was closer than ever to his dream of playing professional football. For him, school football was just a chance to play with his mates and have some fun.

"And no pressure today, Jude," the teacher called from across the room. "Just a hat-trick should be enough for the win."

"What about me?" Odin piped up. "I'm in the Birmingham academy too – it's not all about Jude."

"Very true," laughed the teacher. "So let's see who can score the most."

"Challenge accepted," Jude and Odin both replied, before catching each other's eye and laughing.

Right from the kick-off, the Priory School were on the front foot. Jude and Odin were playing alongside each other in central midfield, and they were bossing the game.

Just a few minutes in, Odin played a one-two with Jude and found himself in space just inside the area. Without looking up, he fired a shot at goal, which crashed off the bar and over.

"Just finding my range. Next one will be top corner," he called over to Jude, who just shook his head in mock disappointment.

The next one was top corner, but it wasn't Jude or Odin with the shot.

The opposition centre-back launched a long ball forward, which bounced straight over the last Priory defender. The centre-forward nipped in behind the defence and fired a clean shot into the goal.

The Priory School were a goal down.

"We could really do with one of those goals right about now, boys," the Priory coach called out, looking pointedly at Odin and Jude.

"Don't worry, it's all under control," Jude replied, still feeling confident.

Jude picked the ball up from the restart and drove forwards, skipping past challenges and using his strength to hold off a defender with ease.

Reaching the edge of the penalty area, he spotted Odin's run and fed the ball into his path. Odin made no mistake this time, and slotted the ball past the keeper, to level the score at 1-1.

"Told you!" laughed Odin.

"Next time, *I'm* being selfish – I can't keep giving you chances on a plate," Jude called back.

For the rest of the half, the pair continued to ping the ball around with ease, but they couldn't score.

The rest of the Priory team weren't quite at Jude's level, so often his perfect through-balls weren't being read, or passes were going astray.

The start of the second half continued in the same way, until a few minutes in, when Jude found himself with the ball at his feet and space to run into.

He turned and accelerated away from his marker, but with the pitch opening up in front of him, his back foot slipped and he fell to the floor, rolling his ankle.

Getting back to his feet, Jude winced and tried to shake it off, but it was obvious that his movement was affected.

His teacher signalled for a substitution.

"Just give me five minutes to see if I can run it off," Jude said, shaking his head in protest.

"I've got to take you off, Jude. Birmingham will already be annoyed that I've let you get injured – they'll be furious if I leave you on," said the teacher.

"Two minutes then – please!" Jude begged. He wanted his goal.

The teacher raised an eyebrow. "Two minutes, Jude. No more. They'd better be the best two minutes of your school career."

From the drop ball, the opposition took control and calmly passed the ball around. Jude tried to chase them down, but he couldn't put much weight on his left foot.

Just then, the ball suddenly bounced loose near the centre circle. Jude turned his body and allowed the ball to drop, so it was goalside. He saw Odin ahead of him, making a run beyond the last defender.

Jude knew he wouldn't be able to control the ball and find the pass. Instead, he just swung his right foot cleanly through the ball and lofted it towards the goal.

The keeper was caught off his line and, in his desperate scramble backwards, he could only watch as the ball sailed over his head and into the top corner.

The Priory players went wild, revelling in such an audacious goal, but Jude just stood still with his arms outstretched, before hobbling off the pitch.

The game finished in a 2-1 win. The Priory School were through to the final, but there was no way Jude would be playing in it.

A week later, the team returned to Bodymoor Heath for the final. Jude was there – but only for moral support.

He was furious to be missing out and wasn't sure if he'd be more annoyed if they won or lost without him.

Jude watched as Odin put Priory 1-0 up, before Odin scored two more, completing his hat-trick and winning the game for the school

Jude tried to celebrate with his friend, but he was gutted not to have been out there with him.

At that moment, Jude vowed he would never watch a final from the sidelines again. He would be out on the pitch, making the difference himself.

Whatever it took.

5
BLUES DEBUT

August 2019, Fratton Park, Portsmouth, England
EFL Cup First Round, Portsmouth v Birmingham City

The first kick of the game went back to David Stockdale in the Birmingham goal.

He launched the ball forward and, as it dropped back down in the centre circle, Jude Bellingham killed the ball with one touch.

He could sense the murmurs of the crowd as he calmly played it off to a team-mate.

Not a bad first touch in professional football, he thought.

The butterflies he'd felt before the game had disappeared into the night sky.

Jude had been training with the Birmingham City first team over the summer, gradually being integrated into the squad. But this was the first cup game of the new season, and he'd been put straight into the starting line-up.

The early exchanges in the game were scrappy, with both teams adjusting to new squads and having to learn each other's style of play.

After half an hour, Portsmouth won a series of corners and Birmingham were struggling to clear their lines.

The third corner in succession was lofted towards the back post, where a header on goal was blocked.

Ellis Harrison, the Portsmouth striker, latched onto the loose ball and forced it goalwards. A despairing Birmingham defender tried to clear it, but the ball had already crossed the line.

It was 1-0 to Portsmouth.

The Birmingham players' heads began to drop.

This was a young team, and many hadn't been in this situation before.

"Heads up boys, keep going!" Jude called out, trying to rally his team-mates. This might be his debut, but he wasn't going to be a passenger.

Minutes later, the ball broke free in the middle of the pitch. Jude picked it up and carried it forward, brushing off a weak challenge.

As he approached the penalty area, an angle opened up and he fired a shot on goal. The keeper scrambled across the line and managed to push it past the post.

Jude couldn't do it all on his own. Not yet.

A few minutes before half-time, Portsmouth had another chance. A well-worked move ended when their winger drilled a shot in on goal, only to see it blocked by the Birmingham defender.

Jude was tracking his runner, Portsmouth's Ben Close, but when the shot was taken Jude paused.

The ball dropped just outside the penalty area and suddenly Ben Close volleyed the ball into the bottom corner.

Portsmouth had their second.

"Jude, that was your runner!" called out Craig Gardner, the experienced Birmingham midfielder.

Jude didn't reply, but he was annoyed at himself for losing concentration and letting Ben Close get that goal. Mistakes were punished so quickly at this level.

At half-time Pep Clotet, the Birmingham manager, called Jude aside for a quiet word.

"You've been our best player out there. Don't lose heart – keep doing what you're doing," he told him. "You're Birmingham's youngest ever player, and I'm glad it was me who gave you that chance. I know this is just the start of something special."

Jude couldn't help but smile. He knew that he'd be supported here, whatever the result. Besides, each mistake was a lesson learned.

Odin Bailey was among the substitutes, still hoping for his debut. He couldn't resist a cheeky dig as Jude went out for the second half.

"Hey, superstar! You'd better do something special to deserve those bright yellow boots."

Jude looked down at his feet, before aiming a playful kick at Odin.

"You won't be doing anything special, sitting on that bench," replied Jude with a grin.

Ten minutes after the restart, Portsmouth put the game to bed.

Their left-winger cut inside onto his right foot and hung a cross up to the back post. Ellis Harrison looped a header past the keeper that nestled just inside the far post.

3-0 to Portsmouth – game over.

Pep Clotet immediately responded by sending on Odin Bailey.

"Just like our old school days," Odin whispered to Jude as he jogged past.

"I wouldn't mind a hat-trick today, if you can manage it," Jude answered.

Just a few minutes later, Jude won the ball on the right wing, before driving to the byline. He fizzed the ball back across the penalty area to where Odin was lurking. Odin swept the ball towards goal, but it narrowly went over the crossbar.

The closing stages of the game were uneventful. The young Birmingham players had expended all their energy and there was to be no comeback on the books.

Jude's race had been run, and he was substituted with 10 minutes to go.

He gestured to the fans as he walked off, and they rose to applaud him.

This had been his first taste of professional football. He hadn't scored and the team had lost — but he'd already learned a lot.

He knew there would be much more to come.

6
COLD NIGHT AGAINST STOKE

August 2019, St. Andrew's, Birmingham, England
Birmingham City v Stoke City

Jude marched confidently out of the tunnel and into the bright lights of St. Andrew's Stadium. He could feel the energy of the crowd as he gazed up at the raucous Tilton Road end.

Thousands of fans were packed in there, cheering the players as they emerged – just as Jude had done so many times as a child.

But today, Jude was here as one of the first-team players.

He had made his league debut in the EFL Championship in Birmingham's previous game, coming on as a late substitute in a 3-0 away defeat to Swansea City.

Today, he was desperate to impress the fans – and his family, who were watching from the stands.

Jude took his place on the bench, wearing his trademark yellow boots and a number 22 shirt.

Thinking about his number made him smile. A couple of years ago, he'd sat down with Mike Dodds, the Head of Development at Birmingham City. They used to have regular chats about how Jude was getting on in the academy.

"Which position do you see yourself playing, if you make it to the first team?" Mike had asked.

"Number 10. I want to be the playmaker, the creator."

Mike had smiled. "So does everyone. And you are great there, Jude. For sure, you'd have a good career as a number 10. But you'd be doing yourself a disservice."

"What do you mean?"

"You can do it all, Jude. You can be a holding midfielder, a box-to-box midfielder, and an attacking midfielder. A number 4, a number 8 and a number 10 – all rolled into one. A number 22!"

Jude had liked that. His eyes had twinkled as he'd considered the possibilities.

"Which top players wear number 22?" he'd asked.

"Jude Bellingham," came the answer.

Jude had spent most of the game against Swansea sitting on the bench alongside Odin Bailey. The pair of them had spent their time analysing the opposition, looking for flaws they could exploit if and when they were subbed on.

Jude had made it on with a quarter of an hour to play, but it hadn't been his 15 minutes of fame, as he'd struggled to make an impact on the game.

For today's game, Odin hadn't been on the team sheet, so Jude was sitting on the bench and watching the game in silence.

The early exchanges of the game all went in Stoke's favour, so Jude settled down, hoping for his chance later in the second half.

Then, after just half an hour, Jefferson Montero, Birmingham's tricky Ecuadorian winger, went down injured, signalling to the bench for a substitution.

Pep Clotet turned to the bench and, after a moment's thought, signalled to Jude. After a few hurried runs up and down the touchline to warm up, Jude was subbed on.

Within minutes, the ball fell kindly to Jude at the edge of the Stoke area. He chopped inside one defender and dragged the ball back to beat another, but was then crowded out by a third, who poked the ball clear.

Without hesitating, he charged after the ball, racing towards the defender on the wing. As the defender went to clear it, Jude launched into a slide tackle and blocked the pass, knocking the ball out for a throw-in.

The Birmingham fans appreciated Jude's energy, rising to their feet and cheering this academy boy who was putting his all into the match.

Just minutes into the second half, Stoke won a free kick on the right wing. They swung a tantalising cross into the box, evading all of the Birmingham defenders. Liam Lindsay was steaming in at the back post and he met the ball with a firm header that flew past the Birmingham keeper.

1-0 to Stoke.

Jude wondered whether this game was going to go the same way as his previous appearances had for City. He'd already had quite enough of losing.

Then, 10 minutes later, the tide turned. Birmingham put together a nice passing move in the middle of the pitch, before spreading the play out to the right wing.

The right-back galloped forward, collecting the pass before hanging a cross up to the back post.

Birmingham's big centre-forward, Lukas Jutkiewicz, met the ball and headed it into the ground, bouncing it up and into the net.

It was 1-1. Game on!

Just three minutes after equalising, a long punt downfield by the Birmingham keeper was headed loose and bounced to Jude in the middle of the pitch. He turned and began to carry the ball towards the Stoke penalty area.

The defenders in front of him parted, tracking runners and leaving a clear path to goal. Jude feinted once to send the last defender in the wrong direction, then fired in a shot from the edge of the box.

The ball clipped the heels of a retreating defender, then looped slowly into the corner of the Stoke net. Jude had put Birmingham in front.

"Goal!" he cried, running over to the home fans. In his excitement he tried a knee slide in celebration, but he just fell on his face. He scrambled up and jumped up with the fans at the Tilton Road end, letting their cheers wash over him as his team-mates piled in too.

He had achieved his dream. He'd become a professional footballer, playing for Birmingham and scoring at St. Andrew's – and he was still only 16 years old. Now he would need to set himself some new goals.

As Jude stood on the pitch, celebrating with his team-mates and the Birmingham fans, he heard the stadium announcer over the loudspeaker.

"Jude Bellingham. Remember the name."

7
ALWAYS A BLUE

July 2020, St. Andrew's, Birmingham, England
Birmingham City v Derby County

It felt as if it was ending before it had even got going.

Just two days ago, Jude had agreed a transfer to Borussia Dortmund, one of the biggest clubs in the German Bundesliga.

That meant that today he was playing for Birmingham for the last time – less than a year after he'd made his debut for the club.

Things seemed to be moving very quickly.

It had been a challenging season for the club, as they'd narrowly avoided relegation to League One.

For all that, Jude had blossomed into the best player in the team, and it had been inevitable that bigger clubs would start paying attention.

As he stood in the tunnel at St. Andrew's, waiting for the rest of the players to line up, Jude looked over at the Derby County players that were beginning to gather next to him.

Among them was Wayne Rooney. He was now in the final years of his career, past his peak. But he was still an awe-inspiring figure – after all, he was Manchester United and England's highest ever goalscorer. And now Jude would be playing against him.

Wayne looked over and caught Jude staring at him.

"I hear you're the most expensive 17-year-old ever," Wayne announced with a grin. "Twenty-five million is a decent fee. I was only twenty million – I think that makes me a bargain."

His smile caught Jude unawares.

"It wasn't anything to do with me," said Jude awkwardly. "I'm only going because the club needs the money."

"There's no need to be humble. You've made the right choice. You don't want to be stuck playing in the Championship any longer than you need to," Rooney replied. "The Champions League is where you belong."

Jude didn't know what to say.

"Anyway, why don't you show me what all the fuss is about?" Rooney added, as the two teams jogged out onto the pitch.

Minutes later, Jude got his chance to do just that. The Birmingham City right-back found himself open on the wing and he drilled a low cross into the Derby area. Jude got to the ball first, taking a touch and making space, before firing a shot at goal. The keeper swatted it away.

"Not bad, not bad," laughed Rooney.

As the players waited for an injury to be dealt with on the pitch, Jude's thoughts went back to Rooney – and his record with Man United. Earlier in the season, when Jude had been looking at his options, he'd actually visited Old Trafford. He'd been given a tour of the ground and had even had a personal talk with Sir Alex Ferguson.

In the end, though, Jude had decided that Man United were unlikely to give him the game time that he was looking for. After all, he'd only played one season of football, and spending a year on the bench – or playing in a youth team somewhere – just wasn't what he was after.

Play restarted and, minutes later, the Birmingham left-back hung a deep cross up to the back post. It was headed back into the box, and Jude brushed past Rooney before crashing a header against the bar. It bounced down and the Derby keeper smothered the ball.

Jude was getting closer.

Shortly after half-time, Jude picked up possession in the middle of the pitch, using his body and his outstretched foot to shield the ball. A Derby player steamed in to challenge for the ball, but was caught by Jude's studs and went down.

Jude looked down and saw that it was Rooney who was on the turf. He was smiling back up at Jude as he held his foot.

"I think you'll do well, kid. Don't show anyone too much respect on a football pitch."

Birmingham equalised shortly after, before Rooney was substituted. Not long after that, Jude too was subbed off.

Jude felt emotional walking off the pitch, at the end of his last game for the club. He'd grown up with Birmingham, starting as a seven-year-old taking his first steps in the academy, then appearing for the first team at the age of just 16.

Due to the social distancing restrictions brought on by the global COVID-19 pandemic, the stands that were usually full of cheering Birmingham fans were empty today. That meant that he couldn't share this moment with the fans.

Even so, he clapped, for all that the club had given him. He would always be a Birmingham fan, wherever his journey took him.

The next day, in training, Craig Gardner called Jude over. Once Jude's team-mate on the pitch, Craig had been named Birmingham's interim manager, after Pep Clotet had left the club just a few weeks earlier.

"The club wanted me to let you know about one last decision they've made," Craig told him.

Jude's heart seemed to miss a beat. Was he going to be told that the transfer was off? Had Dortmund changed their mind?

"Birmingham have decided that they're going to retire your number 22 shirt. Nobody will wear it – until you come back to Birmingham," he said with a broad grin.

Jude was taken aback. "Wait, are they even allowed to do that? I've only played for one season – and we didn't even win anything!"

"Your transfer fee might have saved the club, Jude. We wish you didn't have to go, but it's the best thing for Birmingham City – and for your career," Craig explained.

"But it's not just the money. We all know you will go on to be one of the best players in the world. This gesture is about that," he added. "Besides, you can wear it again when you come back. After all – once a Blue, always a Blue."

8
LIKE A DUCK TO WATER

September 2020, MSV-Arena, Duisburg, Germany
DFB-Pokal First Round, MSV Duisburg v Borussia Dortmund

"I hear you didn't even take a summer holiday this year – just trained. You need to live a little!" Jadon Sancho grinned as he and Jude warmed up before the game.

"I'm seventeen years old, Jadon. I'm sharing a flat with my Mum and I don't speak the language. Football is all I've got!" Jude replied.

"Yeah – I remember that phase," laughed Jadon.

"Don't worry, it passes. You just need me to show you how to enjoy yourself around here."

Jadon Sancho had joined Dortmund at seventeen, and he'd come from England as well, moving from the Man City youth team. That had been three years ago. Now he was one of Dortmund's star players – and an England international as well.

Erling Haaland looked across at the two players and grinned. "Ignore Jadon – he's not going to make you a better player."

"Given I assist most of your goals, I'd have thought you'd be a bit more appreciative," Jadon replied playfully.

Erling Haaland was Dortmund's star striker, a powerful 20-year-old Norwegian who had recently joined from RB Salzburg and was already breaking all sorts of scoring records.

Players like Sancho and Haaland were a big part of the reason why Jude had wanted to join Dortmund. The club had a reputation for turning promising prospects into world-class players, and was known for giving them the game time to prove themselves.

The trio were warming up for the first game of the

season, which was to be Jude's Dortmund debut. And just as at Birmingham, he was playing his first game in the cup.

Jude wasn't feeling in the least bit nervous. This was what he wanted – playing with top players at a top club. He knew he had plenty to contribute on the pitch, and that was all that mattered.

Ten minutes into the game, Jude won a header on the edge of the Duisburg penalty area. The ball broke loose and was played to the Belgian midfielder, Axel Witsel, on the left of the box. He lifted a cross into the area, but it was deflected up and away.

"Handball!" yelled all the Dortmund players as one, as the ball hit a trailing arm of a defender. The referee pointed to the spot.

Jadon grabbed the ball and headed over to the penalty spot to take it.

"If you take this one, I'm having the next!" called out Erling. Jude didn't feel quite ready to argue for penalty rights with two of Dortmund's top players, so he kept quiet.

Jadon stepped up and calmly fired the ball into the top corner.

Jude was the first to celebrate the goal with Jadon. He was less than a quarter of an hour into his first game with Dortmund, but he could already feel that this was a huge step up from Birmingham.

And he was loving it.

Fifteen minutes later, the ball broke free on the right wing and a cross was played into Dortmund's Thorgan Hazard. Jude instantly started to make a run from deep, and Thorgan flicked the ball perfectly into his path.

Jude strode onto the ball, took a touch to set himself and then rolled the ball into the net.

Raising one arm in celebration, he turned and calmly walked away.

"What a goal!" cried Jadon, running straight over to hug Jude. "A goal on your debut – not a bad way to say 'hello' to the fans."

"And that makes you Dortmund's youngest ever scorer," Erling added. "That's one scoring record I can't take back from you!"

Jude just stood on the pitch, a wide grin on his face. He couldn't have imagined a better start than this.

Ten minutes later, Erling ran onto a long ball from

deep, before cleverly dummying it to lose his marker. The defender fell for it completely and, as the last man, chopped Erling down on the edge of the area.

Red card.

Hazard stepped up and fired the resulting free kick into the top corner. It was 3-0 to Dortmund, with the second half still to play.

Jude was subbed off at half-time, to be rested now that the game was clearly won. He looked on from the bench as Giovanni Reyna scored a second-half free kick and then Marco Reus beat the offside trap to slot home goal number five.

Jude Bellingham was happy. Dortmund had won 5-0 on his debut, and in his 45 minutes on the pitch he'd got the second of those goals.

And perhaps most importantly, Dortmund felt like absolutely the right club for him. Things were going to get exciting – he just knew it.

9
THE FIRST OF MANY

November 2020, Wembley Stadium, London, England
International Friendly, England v Republic of Ireland

"Everyone in the family will be so proud," Mark Bellingham announced. "An English grandfather and an Irish grandmother – and it's Ireland you're playing on your England debut. You almost couldn't make this stuff up."

Jude was sitting with his family in his hotel room, on the evening before the game.

"I've got to get on the pitch first, Dad. I'm starting on the bench, remember!" But inwardly, Jude was so pleased to see how much it meant to his dad.

Jude had first played for the England U21 team in September, shortly before his debut for Dortmund. He'd scored on that day too, becoming the youngest player and scorer for England at that level.

"What would you be if you did get on – the youngest-ever England player?" his brother Jobe asked.

"Third youngest. Only Wayne Rooney and Theo Walcott have been younger," Jude replied. He loved football statistics – especially when he was rewriting them himself.

"Until *I* play for England, that is!" Jobe joked.

"You'd better hurry up, Jobe. You're fifteen now – you've only got two years to break my record," Jude shot back.

"Now, now, boys, it's not a competition," Denise added gently.

"It kind of *is* a competition actually, love. That's pretty much the whole point of football," Mark pointed out delicately.

Jude had been called up to the England U21 squad again recently, but injuries to a few players in the senior squad had meant that Gareth Southgate had called him up as a replacement.

The next morning, Jude joined the rest of the squad to travel to Wembley Stadium, leaving his family to cheer from the stands.

Jude sat next to Jadon Sancho on the coach, thinking that a familiar face from Dortmund might help put him at ease.

"You nervous, then?" Jadon asked. "It's a big deal, your England debut."

"You know you're not helping," Jude said, thinking that a joke might help to hide his nerves.

"Oh – you'll be fine, Jude. You might not even get on the pitch. But at least on the bench you'll get a good view of me playing. I mean, best seats in the house!"

Jude was one of the subs for the game, although sitting between Harry Kane and Jordan Henderson was going to be pretty nerve-racking in itself.

A quarter of an hour into the game, a Mason Mount corner was cleared by the Ireland defence to Harry Winks on the edge of the area. He then curled a perfect cross back into the box, which Harry Maguire rose to place in the back of the Ireland net.

Jude jumped up from the bench to celebrate the goal with the rest of the England players. Even so, it still all felt surreal. He felt like a fan, watching most of these players in person for the first time. He knew Jadon of course, and he'd played with Bukayo Saka in the England U21s, but he was more used to seeing the rest of the players on FIFA or Match of the Day.

After half an hour, Jack Grealish found himself in some space on the edge of the Ireland area. He quickly slipped the ball into Jadon on the left-hand side of the area. Sancho waited for the closest defender to come across, before chopping back onto his right foot and firing the ball into the bottom corner of the Ireland goal.

England were now 2-0 up, and Jude knew he would never hear the last of it from Jadon.

Shortly after half-time, Bukayo Saka got the ball on the left wing, but was clipped by a defender in the penalty area as he went by. Dominic Calvert-Lewin stepped up and blasted the resulting penalty into the top corner, giving England an unassailable lead.

Jude immediately recognised that, now the game was won, he was more likely to get a few minutes on the pitch.

Sure enough, ten minutes later, Gareth Southgate waved for Jude to come off the bench and warm up. As Jude ran along the touchline, he looked up at his parents in their box. They waved excitedly, giving him a big thumbs up.

Gareth called him over and put a calming arm around his shoulders. "Just go out there and do what you've done in every other game you've played. Nothing different. This is your first taste – there'll be bigger games to come."

Moments later, Jude was on the pitch, replacing Mason Mount in the England midfield. He was nervous, no doubt, but as soon as he felt the Wembley turf under his feet, and once he'd got his first touch, his nerves all melted away. Now he was just playing football – and he was rather good at that.

10
TROPHY CABINET

May 2021, Olympiastadion, Berlin, Germany
DFB-Pokal Final, RB Leipzig v Borussia Dortmund

"I suppose you've got some wise cracks for me today, then?" Jude said to Jadon.

"Not this time. Today is important business. I've been here four years, and this would be my first trophy," Jadon replied, looking serious for once.

It was the end of Jude's first season in Germany, and today he was walking out to play in a cup final. Dortmund hadn't been able to win the league, with Bayern Munich storming to take the title. So now the German Cup, or DFB-Pokal, offered Dortmund their only chance of silverware, making up for the disappointments in the Bundesliga and the Champions League.

"So four years without a trophy, and now here we are. Seems like I'm what you've been missing, then!" said Jude, keen to keep the tone light.

"That's the attitude," chimed in Erling. "But don't you two worry – I'll do the business today, so you can both start to fill those empty trophy cabinets."

"Hey! I scored in the semi-final, whilst you were injured, and Jadon was nowhere," Jude replied.

"That was against a second division team. I'm just a big-game player, mate," laughed Erling.

Dortmund were up against RB Leipzig, who'd been the third team in the title race. It wasn't going to be an easy final – but then, no final ever was.

The game started quickly, with both teams keen to set the tempo and get an early goal.

After just five minutes, Dortmund won the ball in the middle of the park, and Marco Reus set off a rapid counter-attack. A quick passing move ended with Mahmoud Dahoud slipping the ball into Jadon Sancho on the left of the penalty area. Jadon cut inside, opened his body up and placed the ball in the top corner.

Dortmund had their early lead.

"C'mon, guys, let's go!" Jadon shouted in celebration. "Time for another!"

Twenty minutes later, Reus picked up another loose ball and drove forward, rolling the ball into the path of Erling Haaland. The big Norwegian carried the ball into the box, before using his strength to force the defender, Dayot Upamecano, away from the ball. Erling turned back onto his left foot, then stroked the ball into the net.

Maybe this would be easy after all.

Jude ran to celebrate the goal with Erling and the team. This was turning into the perfect day out. Jude thought back to his last cup final all those years ago, watching his school team from the sidelines. Now he was here playing with Dortmund, as Sancho and Haaland ran riot.

Just before half-time, Marco Reus again ran onto

a through-ball, beating the offside trap. He squared the ball to the onrushing Sancho, who checked inside the last desperate lunge of the defender, before calmly rolling the ball in.

After an anxious wait for VAR to confirm that there was no offside, the goal was given. Not for the first time, Dortmund were 3-0 up, with more than half the game left to play.

"I told you I was in a serious mood today!" Jadon told Jude as they celebrated.

"I wish you were serious more often then, if this is what happens."

With the game won and two more games still to be played in the league, Jude was taken off at half-time.

Seventy minutes into the game, RB Leipzig hit back, with Dani Olmo scoring a goal from 25 yards out.

Any hope of an RB Leipzig comeback was extinguished with just five minutes to go, when Jadon broke free on the right wing and galloped forward.

He played the ball square to Erling, who took a touch, steadied himself, and then slipped and scuffed a bouncing ball towards the goal. The keeper was wrong-footed and, not expecting the slip, somehow let the ball past him. 4-1 to Dortmund.

"That was probably the ugliest goal I've ever seen!" Jadon laughed, as he celebrated with Erling.

"They all count, Jadon. And that's two each – I couldn't have you outscoring me, could I?" Erling grinned.

Minutes later, the final whistle went, and Jude ran onto the pitch to celebrate with the rest of the players. Dortmund were German Cup winners – and Jude had his first trophy, at only seventeen years of age.

A small stage was built on the pitch, and then the Dortmund captain, Marco Reus, lifted the trophy in front of the fans. As fireworks and confetti exploded in the background, Jude cheered and danced with his team-mates, wishing that he could bottle this feeling. He just knew he would have to savour it again and again.

Later, when he finally got his hands on the trophy and held the cold metal tight to his chest, he knew that he didn't want to let go.

II
UNDER THE ARCHES

June 2021, Wembley Stadium, London, England
European Championships Group D, England v Croatia

"So who are you keeping an eye on today?" Jude asked, keen to be prepared if his chance came.

"Luka Modrić," Marcus Rashford answered, straight away. Obviously he'd already thought about it. "He won the Golden Ball for best player at the World Cup, and the Ballon d'Or for best player in the world."

Jude was sitting on the bench with Bukayo Saka and

Marcus Rashford, and they were watching the starting line-up as they filed onto the pitch.

It was a sweltering day, and England were playing Croatia, in a repeat of the World Cup semi-final. That game in 2018 had ended in agonising defeat for England, but today the mood was different.

This was London, for a start. It was a major tournament game at Wembley, for the first time since 1996. Phil Foden had dyed his hair blonde (as Paul Gascoigne had done at the same tournament) and the nation was eager.

Jude Bellingham could sense today's mood – and he thrived on it. He might be on the bench today, but he knew that the Euros was a long tournament. He would get his moment. Even so, he was itching to get a chance to show off today – to the home crowd and to the watching world.

"Modrić, huh?" Jude muttered. "OK, nothing much to worry about there, then."

Bukayo and Marcus just laughed.

"Good luck if you make it onto the pitch," said Bukayo. "We'll stay on the wings and you can handle Modrić in the middle. Deal?"

"Sounds like a plan," said Jude, now serious. He

wanted to make the most of watching Modrić today. He knew he played for Real Madrid, and Jude dreamed of one day pulling on one of their white shirts. Perhaps he could get a step closer to that dream today.

After just a few minutes of play, Kieran Trippier found Raheem Sterling with a long throw-in. Sterling carried the ball down the middle of the park, releasing Phil Foden on the edge of the Croatia area. Then checking inside onto his left foot, Foden crashed a shot against the post and away.

Then, minutes later, Sterling won a corner. It was taken long and the ball fell to Kalvin Phillips at the edge of the area. He controlled a first-time volley at the goal, which the keeper somehow managed to shovel away.

England were showing that they would be no pushover – and Jude found himself sitting on the edge of his seat.

Modrić was still pulling the strings however, and quickly played a neat one-two in the middle of the pitch to make himself some space, before playing a perfect pass down the wing to the Croatia right-back. He played a dangerous cross into the England area, which Ivan Perišić could only blaze over the bar.

Half-time came and went with the score still at 0-0.

Early in the second half, Modrić was at it again. Croatia played the ball across the face of the England box, patiently waiting for space to open up. The ball got played back to Modrić, who took one touch to set himself, before launching a strike on goal, which Pickford scrambled to gather at the second attempt.

While Jude appreciated the quality of the England players, he was beginning to worry that the game was drifting away from them.

He needn't have worried. A few minutes later, Kyle Walker received the ball in the right-back position, before threading a pass into the channel for the onrushing Kalvin Phillips. Phillips checked inside his defender, riding the last-ditch challenge. He played a perfect through-ball to Raheem Sterling, who managed to prod the ball over the keeper and into the net.

1-0 to England – and Wembley was bouncing.

A little while later, Gareth Southgate turned to his subs bench, paused for a moment, then called Jude over to the touchline.

"Get out there and put pressure on their midfield,

Jude. They've been running for 80 minutes in this heat – they're tired. Modrić isn't as young as he once was – you can limit his influence."

Southgate's confidence gave Jude confidence. This wasn't a cap for the sake of it, for experience. This was tournament football, and Jude was coming on to do a job for his team and his country, against one of the best players in the world.

Straight away, Jude was amongst the action, chasing down long balls and harrying the Croatia midfield. As long as he was on the pitch, he told himself, Croatia wouldn't get back into the game.

Moments later, a Croatia player gathered the ball and ran towards the England defence. Jude raced after him and, sensing a moment's hesitation, launched into a sliding tackle. He took the ball cleanly, and followed through on the man, making it clear whose ball it was.

"Good tackle," was all Luka Modrić said, after picking himself up off the turf.

With just a few moments to go, and with England still holding on by a single goal, Croatia won a free kick in a dangerous spot. The ball was swung in towards the area and Domagoj Vida, the bruising Croatia centre-back, climbed into the air to meet it. Jude also leapt up, desperate to reach the ball first.

The two players clashed heads with a loud, sickening thump, then they both fell to the ground. The physios rushed on to treat them, but both players were gingerly back on their feet after a few seconds.

One thing was certain – Jude wasn't going to be bullied by anyone.

There were no further goals in the game, so the final whistle saw England celebrating winning their opening game of the tournament. Gareth Southgate ruffled Jude's hair as the players celebrated on the pitch.

"You know, that made you the youngest-ever player from any nation to play in the European Championship," Gareth said, smiling. "That's quite the record!"

"I've had enough records for being the youngest at stuff. From now on, I want them to be about me being the best!"

Gareth laughed. "I wouldn't worry about that. Being the best will come soon enough. And hopefully it'll bring a trophy for England along with it."

12
THE BRIDESMAID

July 2021, Wembley Stadium, London, England
European Championships Final, England v Italy

It was the European Championship final, at Wembley, and England were playing, in their first major tournament final since 1966. With the scores locked at 0-0, there were just minutes remaining. It was time for someone to make themselves a hero.

Jude looked at the wide Wembley pitch opening up in front of him, the green grass brilliant under the bright sun.

He walked over to his starting position, in the middle of the England midfield.

The ball was lofted through the air, and Jude's eye followed the arc of the ball, before he fired a perfect volley into the back of the net. The crowd roared their delight, and Jude spread his arms wide as he took in their appreciation.

England had won the cup – and Jude had won it for them.

"Hey! Stop daydreaming, Jude. Time to head out," Jadon Sancho grinned, giving his friend a shove.

"It's not daydreaming – it's visualisation. I like to know where I'm going to be, the situations that might happen. That way, I'm ready for anything that comes," Jude replied.

It was the Euros final, at Wembley, and England were playing. So far, that part of Jude's visualisation had come true.

Jadon and Jude were both starting on the bench, and they took their seats alongside Bukayo Saka and Marcus Rashford.

After the Croatia game, Jude had come on against the Czech Republic in the group stage, and in the quarter-final against Ukraine. England had stormed to the final, even beating old enemies Germany in the round of 16, and many fans felt that this was their time. The players could feel the expectation in the stadium.

Jude hadn't expected to be starting in the final, but he was sure he would come on. He wasn't here for experience – he was here to help make this happen, to contribute in the big moments. And moments didn't come much bigger than this.

Just two minutes into the game, Harry Kane picked up the ball from deep and spread it wide to the right. Kieran Trippier picked it up in space and paused as runners piled into the box. He hung a deep cross up to the back post, past the Italy right back.

Luke Shaw strode onto the ball, before connecting with a sweet half-volley, which kissed the left-hand post on its way into the back of the net.

Two minutes in, 1-0 up – the perfect start. The stadium erupted as the England fans celebrated the early lead with the players. Already it felt as if England had one hand on the trophy.

The rest of the first half was cagey. England were content with their lead, not wanting to take too many risks. Italy weren't willing to push forward too hard and risk conceding another goal – although they still managed a few half-chances, with Federico Chiesa and Marco Verratti both testing Jordan Pickford in the England goal.

Jude spent the first half watching Italy's midfield carefully, looking for any weaknesses. And any time an England player went down, a small part of him hoped that they'd have to come off, just so he could get on.

"No changes, keep doing what you've been doing so far," Gareth Southgate told his players at half-time. "We're winning. Let's keep it that way."

In the second half, Italy seemed to have all the momentum. Chiesa had another chance and, after twenty minutes, Italy won a corner.

The ball was lofted in and England struggled to clear their lines. Leonardo Bonucci, the big Italy centre-back, fought his way to the loose ball and fired it into the back of the net, bringing Italy level.

As the England fans in the stadium fell silent, Gareth Southgate turned to his bench and called for a player to come down to warm up. Jude was sure it would be him, but then Bukayo Saka brushed past on his way down.

The game ticked on, with neither team finding a way through. England brought on a midfielder for fresh legs, but it wasn't Jude – it was Jordan Henderson.

Jude stayed positive, sure that eventually he would get on and score the winner. England still had three subs left – plenty of time and opportunity. He stretched out his legs, keen to be ready whenever needed.

With just a few moments left of the 90 minutes, Saka won the ball on the right wing and prodded it past the veteran Giorgio Chiellini in the Italy defence, putting him clear through on the flank. Chiellini grabbed Saka's shirt and pulled him down to the floor.

"Foul!" cried Jude, along with the rest of the bench. The Italy players were renowned for their strong defence and, this time, although Chiellini received a yellow card, Saka's attack had been neutralised.

Extra time started, and soon afterwards Jack Grealish was subbed on. Rashford, Sancho and Jude all started looking at each other on the bench. Only two more substitutes left, and 30 minutes for somebody to become a hero. Or a villain.

The minutes of extra time ticked down with neither

team able to take advantage. Then, just before the final whistle, Gareth Southgate turned to his bench for the last time.

By this time, Jude was already visualising penalties. He'd decided he would go for the bottom-right corner, and he'd already taken it a thousand times in his mind. He was sure Southgate was about to call him down.

"Marcus, you're on," Southgate called. Gareth looked at the bench one more time, before beckoning his final substitute. "Jadon, you too."

Jude's stomach lurched. He wasn't going to get to play. Not a single minute. England's biggest game in his lifetime and, win or lose, he wasn't going to have any impact on the game.

He was devastated, but he put on a brave face. This was a team game, and they would win or lose as a team.

The game went to penalties and they seemed to go on forever. The tension in the stadium, amongst the players and fans alike, was unbearable. Berardi scored for Italy, before Harry Kane fired it in for England. 1-1 after the first round.

Belotti's penalty was brilliantly saved by Pickford,

before Maguire smashed his penalty into the top corner. 2-1 and advantage to England.

Bonucci, already Italy's hero, stepped up and scored. Then Marcus Rashford agonisingly hit the post and wide. 2-2.

Bernardeschi scored easily, before Jadon Sancho stepped up. Jude had seen Jadon score so many penalties for Dortmund, he knew that the ball was as good as in the net.

He was wrong. Donnarumma saved it, making it 3-2 to Italy. It was all going wrong.

Then Jorginho missed for Italy, giving England a chance to come back. Bukayo Saka just had to score to go to sudden death. But his penalty was tame and Donnarumma dived to save it.

Italy had won the Euros.

Jude was heartbroken. Heartbroken for his friends, knowing how terrible they would feel. And for himself, for not getting his chance, for helplessly having to watch it all unfold.

He felt lost.

13
BRACE YOURSELF

October 2022, Westfalenstadion, Dortmund, Germany
Borussia Dortmund v Stuttgart

Just two minutes into the game, Jude received the ball on the edge of the Stuttgart area. He laid it off to the right, where Niklas Süle was arriving from full-back. Süle played the ball square into the box and Jude strode onto the return pass, before stroking the ball calmly past the keeper and in. Goal!

Jude ran to the Südtribüne, the huge all-standing

terrace in the Dortmund stadium, before spreading his arms to take in the adulation. He listened to the 80,000 fans all roaring their appreciation – a far cry from the empty stadiums he'd started his career in.

It was now more than a year since the disappointment of the Euros final and, at Dortmund, Jude was now the star of the show. Jadon Sancho had left for Man United shortly after that final, and Erling Haaland had gone to Man City a year later.

Dortmund had come second in the league last year – once again to Bayern. This year, they were determined to break that streak and add the league to their silverware. That meant that a win today, against Stuttgart, was essential if they were to keep up the pressure on Bayern.

They only had four games after today's game before an early winter break, enforced by the move of the 2022 World Cup to November and December, to avoid the summer heat of Qatar, where the tournament was being held.

Ten minutes further into the game, Dortmund won a free kick, deep in the Stuttgart half. The ball was swept into the box and Süle deftly steered it into the back of the net. Dortmund were flying.

Just before half-time, Giovanni Reyna picked up a pass on the corner of the area, before cutting inside onto his right foot and firing the ball into the bottom corner. 3-0 Dortmund.

At half-time, the captain usually said a few words to the players. Earlier that month, in the absence of Marco Reus through injury, Jude had taken up the captaincy of Dortmund for the first time, at the age of just 19. He was the youngest ever captain in the Bundesliga, for any team. But it didn't show.

"That's more like it, boys. This is how we play when we are at our best. So I want more of the same in the second half, to secure the win and send a signal," he yelled, clapping to keep the tempo high.

"We're all thinking about the World Cup in a few weeks' time – this is our final audition. A big win, a few goals … then we're going into the biggest tournament as in-form players. If you don't do it for anyone else, do it to get yourself on the plane to Qatar!"

Despite his youth, Jude understood football and he

understood players. He'd been to a major tournament before, but this time he would be going as a key first-team player. He was now regularly starting games for England and was feeling so much stronger, with the confidence of a leader at the highest level.

Just five minutes into the second half, Jude displayed that confidence for all to see. He came onto the ball in the middle of the park, facing his own goal. He pirouetted easily away from his marker and drove at the Stuttgart box.

The defenders parted in front of him, unsure whether to close him down. Jude took advantage of their hesitation and curled a beautiful strike into the top corner.

4-0 to Dortmund, and Jude was in charge. He didn't need to cheer or shout, he just silently opened his arms to the crowd and let their enthusiasm wash over him. He was the entertainer and this was his stage.

Goalscoring was a recent addition to his game. Previously his focus had been on dictating the play from midfield, but this season he was Dortmund's top scorer. He'd scored in each of their four matches in the Champions League so far, as well.

Ten minutes later, Jude was at it again. He picked up the ball from deep, before driving forward and playing an inch-perfect pass into the left channel for the onrushing Raphaël Guerreiro, who squared the ball for Youssoufa Moukoko to tap it into the open net.

5-0 to Dortmund. The Dortmund players were sending a message – to Bayern, and to the national teams readying for Qatar.

Jude felt more than ready. He was now into his third season at Dortmund and was on top of his game. The World Cup was arriving at the perfect time.

14
ON THE WORLD STAGE

November 2022, Khalifa International Stadium, Doha, Qatar
World Cup Group B, England v Iran

Jude walked out into the burning sun, head held high as he took his first steps onto the pitch at the World Cup. Even though the tournament had been moved to Qatar's winter, it was still hot by English standards. Their opposition, Iran, would be much more comfortable.

Widely tipped to be one of the best young players at the tournament and therefore in the world, Jude was getting a start today. He had come a long way since the last major tournament, 18 months ago, and this time he was determined to make a difference.

"You know, this is my chance to put things right after missing that penalty against Italy," Bukayo said as he walked alongside Jude.

"You don't need to put anything right, Bukayo. You did your best – everyone knows that," Jude replied. "Plus, I didn't even get on the pitch, so I can't criticise! So today, let's treat this as just another game to show what we can do. Even if it's already 30 degrees."

Jude proudly belted out the national anthem as the players lined up. This was his stage, representing his country at the World Cup. He had a job to do.

The game started fairly slowly, with Iran pressing and challenging hard. England moved the ball around calmly, waiting for an opportunity, keen not to tire themselves out too quickly in the heat.

After half an hour of patient play, Raheem Sterling picked the ball up in the middle of the pitch, before laying it into the path of Luke Shaw, who floated a delicate cross into the middle of the Iran penalty area.

Jude was waiting for it and rose gracefully, glancing the ball into the top corner with a header.

England had the lead, and Jude had his first international goal.

Jude ran to the corner flag, pumping his fist in celebration with the England fans. He knew his parents were in the crowd too – he hoped that they were enjoying the moment as much as he was.

"What a way to make an impression!" Bukayo laughed, joining in the celebration.

"Now it's your turn to banish some demons!" Jude replied.

Ten minutes later, a Luke Shaw corner was headed down by Harry Maguire and the ball bounced loose in the Iran penalty area. Bukayo strode onto the ball and fired it into the back of the net, clipping the crossbar as it sailed in.

2-0 England.

"Just like that!" grinned Jude. "You almost took the net off!"

Saka smiled, the weight of that missed penalty against Italy now off his shoulders.

A few minutes later, Bukayo was fouled near the half-way line, but the ball broke for Jude. With the referee signalling for advantage, he carried the ball forward, riding two challenges from Iran defenders before slipping the ball into the space he had created for Harry Kane.

Kane swept an inch-perfect ball across the face of the goal, and Raheem Sterling arrived just in time, prodding the ball past the keeper and in.

England were flying – a perfect start to their World Cup.

A little while into the second half, Sterling played the ball into Saka on the edge of the Iran area. He checked inside, then checked again and again, looking for space. Eventually an angle opened up, and he slotted the ball straight into the bottom corner.

4-0 England.

"Didn't you see my run?" Jude joked as he celebrated with Bukayo. "I was wide open!"

Iran snuck a goal back a few minutes later, but England hadn't finished yet.

Marcus Rashford was subbed on and, just seconds

later, a long ball was brilliantly controlled by Harry Kane, who immediately found Rashford, giving him his first touch.

Marcus chopped inside the defender, and rolled the ball past the keeper and in.

Then, with just a few minutes to go, Jude won the ball back in the middle of the park, brushing off a tired Iran defender. He played a perfect through-ball to Callum Wilson, who in turn played a square pass to Jack Grealish, who tapped it in.

England had six. Even another late consolation for Iran couldn't dampen the mood.

England had clearly announced their intentions at this World Cup, and Jude Bellingham had stamped his name all over the game.

He was here, and he meant business.

15
ONE DAY

December 2022, Al Bayt Stadium, Al Khor, Qatar
World Cup Quarter-Final, England v France

"I've got to get one, H," Jude said to Harry Kane as they sat in the coach on the way to the stadium. "I need to win a World Cup – or a Euros. There's only three more games."

"You've got plenty of time, Jude – you're only 19. I'll be nearly 33 by the time the next World Cup comes around. This might be my last chance."

"Yeah, but I've had enough of near misses and second places. It's time to start winning something," Jude answered grimly.

"That's the right attitude." Harry looked up at Jude. "Winning trophies isn't everything – you've got plenty of records already. But that hunger is really important. And you can't win trophies on your own. Otherwise maybe you should have been a runner or tennis player!"

"Ignore Harry," chipped in Marcus Rashford. "He might score the odd goal, but he definitely doesn't know anything about winning trophies!"

England had cruised into the quarter-finals, beating Senegal 3-0 in the round of 16 after topping their group. Now they were up against France, the reigning world champions. They were a big step up compared to any team England had faced so far, with the likes of Kylian Mbappé in their squad.

The game started quickly, with France immediately getting at England and zipping the ball around at pace. After just a few minutes, Antoine Griezmann carried the ball forward and slipped it into Ousmane Dembélé on the right wing, who curled in a first-time cross to

Olivier Giroud. His header was straight at Pickford in the England goal.

England didn't heed the warning and, minutes later, Dembélé had the ball on the right wing again, facing up against the retreating England defence. A square ball ended up at the feet of Aurélien Tchouaméni. Jude raced out to close the ball down, but got there too late, as Tchouaméni fired the ball into the back of the England net from 25 yards out.

1-0 France.

"Sorry, boys. I should have closed him down quicker," Jude called over, as the England players watched France celebrate.

"You did more than anyone else. Heads up, lots more football to play!" said Harry, consoling Jude.

England responded well to going behind. Minutes later, Harry rolled his defender expertly and ended up through on goal, but his shot was saved and Jude couldn't quite force the rebound into the back of the net.

Harry Kane seemed to be everywhere. Again he span his defender, but was heavily brought down inside the area. Somehow, the referee didn't blow for a penalty. Then minutes later, Kane fired in a shot from distance, which only a despairing dive from Hugo Lloris in the France goal could keep out.

As the game ticked over into the second half, England continued to dominate. A Phil Foden corner dropped to Jude on the edge of the France area. He drove in a fierce first-time half-volley, which the keeper only just managed to tip away.

"Keep going, Jude – it's coming!" Harry called, reassuringly.

Just a few minutes later, it came. Bukayo Saka picked up the ball on the right wing, before driving into the penalty area. He played a quick one-two with Jude, before being clumsily taken down by Tchouaméni. The penalty was awarded to England and Kane stepped up to fire it home.

England were level, and now they were in the ascendancy.

Even though they had more of the ball, the quality of the France players meant that England could never relax. With just fifteen minutes to go, Griezmann picked up the ball on the left wing, before floating a perfect cross into the England near post. Giroud was lurking, and he stooped to head the ball cleanly into the back of the England net.

France were one up.

With a quarter of an hour to find the goal, England had to respond – and Jude was determined to make his impact. This had to be his time.

With only five minutes to go, he picked up the ball on the half-way line and, out of the corner of his eye, spotted the run of Mason Mount. He played an inch-perfect diagonal ball over the defence, but as Mount was about to reach it, he was barged over by Theo Hernández.

"Penalty!" cried the England players in unison – but the referee did not agree. Then, thanks to VAR, he was called back to view it again on the monitor. After a few agonising minutes, he changed his mind and awarded the penalty.

Harry Kane stepped up. Jude felt calm. He had seen Harry score these so many times, in training as well as in matches. Jude was already thinking about how, after

Harry levelled the score, *he* would get a late winner and make himself the hero.

Harry stepped up ... and blazed it wildly over the bar. The England players and fans all gasped in shock. England's one penalty-taker who never missed – had missed.

England had one last chance before the final whistle – a free kick that Marcus Rashford put narrowly over the bar. Now there was no way back.

At the final whistle, Jude slumped to the ground in despair. He had lost. England had lost.

His thoughts went back to the conversation he'd had with Harry Kane on the coach, on the way to the match. Wiping his tears from his eyes, Jude went over and consoled Harry, who he knew would be feeling terrible, knowing that if he'd scored, England would still be in the game.

Even in these darkest moments, Jude knew that he was part of a team. They needed to support each other – and, right now, it was Harry that needed his support.

16
SO CLOSE

May 2023, Westfalenstadion, Dortmund, Germany
Borussia Dortmund v Mainz 05

Ninety minutes. That was all that stood between Jude Bellingham and his first-ever league title. It would also be Dortmund's first Bundesliga win in over a decade.

If they could manage it. They were two points clear of Bayern Munich at the top of the table, with just today's games to go. Even though their goal difference was much worse, if Bayern won today, against FC Köln, all Dortmund had to do was win against Mainz and the trophy was theirs. If Bayern didn't win, they could draw or even lose and still win the title.

It all sounded so simple.

To add to the drama, the Dortmund and Bayern games were both kicking off at the same time, so there would be plenty of internet traffic as each team kept a close eye on the other team's score.

Just to add to Jude's nerves, he was injured. He'd been having knee problems in the latter part of the season and, even though he was on the bench today, there was no way he'd be able to play.

As he took his seat on the bench, Jude opened the live scores page for Bayern on his phone. Giovanni Reyna was sitting next to him on the bench. Unlike Jude, Gio was hoping to get on the pitch.

"Let me know if Bayern score, Jude," he said.

"You just worry about winning this game. Then it won't matter," Jude replied, the frustration and tension obvious to hear in his voice. He trusted his team-mates, but deep down he thought they would have a better chance with him on the pitch.

The game kicked off, and Jude was comforted by the fact that, as it stood, Dortmund were winning the title. If nothing else happened in the next two hours, they were home and dry.

That comfort didn't last long. Just eight minutes into the game, his phone updated. Kingsley Coman had scored for Bayern Munich. Gio Reyna looked over Jude's shoulder and sighed deeply.

"Still got plenty of time. Just need a goal here and we're fine," Jude muttered, feigning confidence.

The goal came only minutes later, but it wasn't Dortmund who scored. Mainz won a corner and Edimilson Fernandes swung the ball into the near post, where Mainz's big Norwegian centre-back Andreas Hanche-Olsen stooped to head it past the keeper.

Mainz had the lead – and 80,000 Dortmund fans were stunned into silence. The home team now needed two goals to win the league.

Just a minute later, Raphaël Guerreiro was clattered in the Mainz box, and Dortmund were awarded a penalty. Jude felt relieved. After a bad start, they could now get back level, needing just one more goal.

Sébastien Haller stepped up to take the kick, but stuttered during the run-up and fired a tame penalty at waist height, which the keeper easily saved.

Jude couldn't believe what he was seeing. It never seemed to go his way in these critical matches.

Five minutes later, Mainz got a man free on the left wing, and the resulting cross was headed in by Karim Onisiwo. Mainz now had a two-goal lead, and it seemed a long way back for Dortmund.

Jude might not be able to play, but he wasn't going to just sit by and watch it happen. He jumped up and strode over to the edge of the pitch.

"Come on, boys!" he called out. "This isn't good enough. This isn't us! Don't end today with any regrets, this is a chance we might never get again!"

The players responded to his energy, seeing that if an injured Jude could show some passion from the bench, they should be able to match it on the pitch.

Half-time came and went, and shortly afterwards Gio Reyna got stripped off and ready to come on. Dortmund needed a spark.

"Their right-back is leaving some space inside.

Make sure you make the most of it," Jude whispered, as Gio walked down past him. Gio nodded in response, knowing that Jude would have been watching for any weaknesses in the opposition.

Five minutes later, Reyna picked up the ball and drove forward, cutting inside from the left wing and playing a one-two with Raphaël Guerreiro, who slid the return pass into the back of the net.

Now there was only a one-goal deficit, and the Dortmund players looked as if they had life back in their challenge.

Ten minutes later, Jude's phone buzzed again. He'd almost forgotten about the other match, but now he was glad to be reminded. Dejan Ljubičić had just scored for FC Köln, making it 1-1.

Jude showed his team-mates, and the news quickly rippled around the ground. As it stood, Bayern had closed the gap to a point, but Dortmund were back to being champions-in-waiting.

Jude settled down to watch the rest of the game – then his phone buzzed again. He looked down and saw the name of his friend Jamal Musiala. They had played together for England U17s, before Jamal had committed to Germany, but this time it wasn't good news. Musiala had just scored for Bayern, putting them 2-1 up.

The pendulum had swung back in Bayern's favour. Dortmund had five minutes to score twice.

Just like the rest of the game, it didn't seem to be quite happening for Dortmund. Then, with just seconds to go, Reyna flicked on a cross into the Mainz box, and Niklas Süle juggled the ball twice before firing it into the back of the net.

Dortmund had levelled, but still needed another in the dying seconds to win the league.

A minute more was played, which was only enough for Mainz to keep possession from the kick-off, before the referee's shrill whistle echoed around the stadium.

Dortmund's players fell to the ground in despair, and Jude hobbled down from the bench to be with them. He had fallen short again, at the very last hurdle.

This was becoming a habit – and Jude hated it.

17
THE NEXT GALÁCTICO

June 2023, Ciudad Real Madrid, Madrid, Spain

Jude stood there, transfixed, just staring at the fourteen glistening Champions League trophies. He wanted to reach out and touch them, to hold one aloft.

"This way, Jude," said Florentino Pérez, the president of Real Madrid, gesturing to the long table that dominated the boardroom.

Jude walked up slowly and took a seat, with his dad,

his mum and brother Jobe standing close behind. Nobody said anything, but his mum gently squeezed his hand. Jude's contract to play for Real Madrid lay on the table, open at the right page. All it needed was his signature.

The transfer negotiations had been going on for some time. There was a lot to discuss with such a big fee – 88 million pounds, rising to 115 million, depending on Jude's performance. Jude hoped that he'd be good enough to make them pay every penny of that.

Jude had said goodbye to his Dortmund team-mates on the day after they had lost the league title. He'd known he'd be leaving, long before it was all publicly confirmed. Jude knew it was the right thing to do, but leaving Germany was still very emotional. It was where he had become a man – and where he'd become the player that Real Madrid wanted to spend so much money on.

A few days after his goodbyes, Jude had received the Player of the Year award at the Bundesliga end of season awards ceremony.

"Not the award for Young Player of the Year? I'm only nineteen," Jude had asked in surprise.

So now Jude's family watched as he signed on the

dotted line. He was now a Real Madrid player, for the next six years.

After the signing, Jude was given his Real Madrid shirt. This was the first shirt of his career that didn't have his number 22 on the back. Instead, he would wear the number 5. Jude had chosen it as it was the number worn by one of his heroes, the great Zinedine Zidane. Any player who wore that shirt would feel the weight of history but, for Jude, it was just a greater motivation to impress.

In the press conference that followed, Pérez was first to speak. "Today is a very exciting day for Madridistas, because one of the best players in the world has come to Real Madrid."

In recent years, Jude had heard many fans and pundits call him one of the best players in the world, and he'd never taken it seriously. But hearing it from the president of Real Madrid was different. A small part of him was still surprised that Pérez even knew who he was.

When it was Jude's turn to speak, he kept it short and sweet. "Thank you all for joining me today for the best day of my life, when I join the greatest football club in the history of the game."

He looked over at his family and thought he could see a tear in his dad's eye. His dad never cried.

"Keep it together, old man," Jude whispered as he sat back down. "Don't want to be blubbing in front of the world's media."

A few minutes later, Jude got the chance to wear his new shirt for the first time. He slipped the crisp, all-white shirt over his head and felt the badge pressing against his chest. It wasn't a weight – it was a source of energy.

With the Real Madrid stadium, the Santiago Bernabéu, closed due to renovations, Jude walked out instead onto Real's training pitch.

He was already visualising walking out at the Santiago Bernabéu for his first game, surrounded by the roar of the fans.

Jude had arrived. This was the very first day of his life at the very pinnacle of professional football. There was nowhere higher that he could go. He would be playing alongside and against the best players in the world, with all the pressure and expectation that came with that.

He couldn't wait.

18
HEY JUDE

October 2023, Estadi Olímpic Lluís Companys, Barcelona, Spain
Barcelona v Real Madrid

"You'll force me into retirement, you know," Luka Modrić grinned, as the pair of them warmed up together.

"You'd better teach me all your tricks then, before you go!" Jude laughed.

Jude still couldn't quite believe he was here. He remembered feeling awestruck playing against Modrić, just two years ago in the Euros, and now here they were, as team-mates. Except that Jude's start in Madrid had been so impressive that, today, Modrić was on the bench for the first Clásico of the season.

"If I make it onto the pitch today, it'll be my 500th game for Real Madrid," Luka said, as focused and as professional as ever.

"Not bad! I only need 490 more to catch you up, then. Look – if it's getting late in the game and you haven't made it on, I'll just pretend I've got cramp. You need to get that record in the Clásico, Luka, it's only fitting."

Jude had made an electric start to his season. After scoring 14 goals in the whole of last season for Dortmund, he'd scored 11 goals in his first 12 games with Real. He was scoring so many, he was already being compared to Cristiano Ronaldo.

Jude was very aware of the importance of El Clásico in Spanish football, and he could remember watching it as a boy, at home with his family. Today was his chance to see it, to play in it and to make some history of his own.

The game was being held in the Olympic Stadium in Barcelona, rather than in their usual stadium, the Camp Nou, which was undergoing renovations. Even so, he knew there would still be 50,000 screaming Barcelona fans in the ground, and millions around the world watching.

Just six minutes into the game, it all went wrong. Barcelona played a couple of short passes in the middle of the park, in their typical tiki-taka style. Aurélien Tchouaméni stuck a foot in to break up the play, but accidentally knocked the ball towards his own goal. Antonio Rüdiger slid in to intercept, but he could only bounce the ball into the path of İlkay Gündoğan, who calmly stroked the ball into the back of the net.

1-0 to Barcelona, and the stadium was bouncing.

"Come on boys, let's lift it!" Jude called to his team-mates. Just as at Birmingham and Dortmund, it hadn't taken him long to become a leader on the pitch.

Barcelona remained on top, though, and even Jude was finding it tricky in the middle of the park, up against Gündoğan and Barcelona's own teenage prodigy, Gavi.

Shortly after half-time, a header from Barcelona's Iñigo Martínez crashed against the Real Madrid post. Ronald Araújo followed up with a shot on the rebound for Barça, which Kepa Arrizabalaga in the Real Madrid goal just managed to keep out.

After an hour, the Real Madrid manager, Carlo Ancelotti, made a change. On came Luka Modrić, getting his 500th appearance – in El Clásico.

"You look like you could do with a hand here," he said to Jude with a smile.

"I was just waiting until you were here to witness the Bellingham show up close!" Jude joked. Despite the difficult game so far, he was still confident that they could turn this around.

Five minutes later, a deep cross into the Barcelona box was headed out to the edge of the area. Jude ran after the ball and collected it facing his own goal. He quickly turned and opened up his body, before unleashing an unstoppable drive into the top corner from a full 25 yards out.

1-1. All square again.

"Get in!" Jude cried, waving to the small stand of travelling Real Madrid fans, wanting them to make more noise.

He was delighted, but he knew that they needed to push on for the win. It was a great goal, but great goals get forgotten if the game is lost.

"Not bad, Jude. Me being on the pitch has obviously made all the difference!" Luka Modrić grinned as the two trotted back to their half for kick-off.

The next half an hour proved frustrating, as Real Madrid couldn't find the space for a clear-cut chance and the teams seemed equally matched. As the match drifted into injury time, Jude began to think that his first Clásico might end in stalemate.

Then, with just a minute of stoppage time left, Dani Carvajal looped in a hopeful cross from the right. Modrić reached the ball first and flicked it onwards, past the last Barcelona defender. Jude timed his run perfectly and snuck in behind the defender, before half-volleying the ball past the keeper from point-blank range.

With seconds to go, he had put Real Madrid in front. Jude sprinted to the corner flag, where he stood, arms outstretched, nodding at the fans. He took the booing from the Barça fans together with the applause and the cheers from the Real fans.

He was here, and he was in charge.

"Job done," he said to himself calmly.

19
GOLDEN BOY

October 2023, Théâtre du Châtelet, Paris, France
Ballon d'Or Award Ceremony

Jude Bellingham, the boy from Stourbridge, sat in the back of the taxi as it sped quietly through the streets of Paris. He had arrived not long before on a business class flight from Madrid and was here for one night only. Dressed in black tie, he obviously wasn't here on holiday.

Bringing him back to earth were his parents, sitting on either side of him in the taxi, like slightly disappointing bodyguards. His brother, Jobe, was back in England, himself now a professional football player, with all the structure and discipline that that required.

The car swept up to the entrance of the opera house and Jude stepped out onto the red carpet.

"Jude! Jude! Over here!" cried the photographers, trying to get the best shot of each player as they arrived.

"How does it feel to be here, at the Ballon d'Or ceremony – with the best players in the world?" Jude was asked by a journalist.

"It's an honour just to be here, to be honest," replied Jude, who turned to see David Beckham and Lionel Messi walking inside.

Jude took his seat in the front row, next to his club team-mate Vinícius Júnior, and looked around in awe. It didn't feel like *that* long ago that he'd been playing with school friends in the Birmingham academy – yet now he was here, with the best players in the world. And he was one of them.

He thought ahead to the end of the season. Real Madrid went into every competition expecting to win it, and Jude was already thinking about winning La Liga.

After losing out to Bayern in his final days at Dortmund, Jude was desperate to win a league title.

But the Champions League was the one he really wanted. Ever since signing his contract in the shadow of the fourteen trophies that Real Madrid had already won, he had dreamt of holding aloft the fifteenth.

Then, once his club football was done and dusted, Jude had the small matter of representing England at the European Championships, that summer in Germany, to look forward to. After the disappointments he'd experienced against France and Italy in previous tournaments, he was determined to make it third time lucky.

His thoughts were interrupted by Eden Hazard, who was walking onto the stage to announce the next award, the Kopa Trophy. This was the award for the best U21 player in the world – and Jude had been nominated, alongside his friend, Jamal Musiala, and players like Gavi at Barcelona.

Jude waited as Hazard opened the golden envelope and took out the card bearing the winner's name.

"Jude Bellingham."

Jude strode up onto the stage, smiling widely, and shook hands with the host, Didier Drogba, before accepting the golden trophy from Hazard.

Then he said a few words, as was customary.

"I just want to thank everyone who has helped me get to this point – from Birmingham City to Borussia Dortmund, and now Real Madrid and the national team. And, most importantly, thanks to my family – my mum and dad, who are here tonight, and my brother watching back home. Thank you for the support, it means so much."

As Jude walked back to his seat, he tried to enjoy the moment, to savour this stunning achievement.

But he was Jude Bellingham, and that meant that he was already thinking about La Liga, the Champions League – and the rest of the silverware that he knew would be coming his way.

20
HALA MADRID

May 2024, Estadio Santiago Bernabéu, Madrid, Spain
Real Madrid v Cadiz

"This is the game, guys, I can feel it," said Luka Modrić. He continued tying his laces, not looking up but knowing that everyone in the dressing room was thinking about the same thing.

"That's easy for you to say. At least you're starting – you can make a difference," Jude said quietly, looking at Luka, who was sitting beside him.

Real Madrid were on the brink of sealing the La Liga title. All they needed to do was beat Cadiz today – and hope that Barcelona wouldn't beat Girona.

Jude had mixed feelings. He was excited to be on the verge of his first-ever league title, but today he was starting on the bench, which meant that he wasn't where he wanted to be – on the pitch, making things happen.

"The gaffer will sub you on if we need you," Luka grinned. "You're our not-so-secret weapon, lurking there on the bench."

Luka was right. Jude understood why he was a sub today – and it wasn't because he'd been playing badly. In the months since he'd won his Kopa Trophy at the Ballon d'Or ceremony, he'd shown no signs of slowing down on the pitch.

In January, he'd won his first silverware for Real Madrid, winning the Spanish Super Cup, beating Barcelona 4-1 in the final.

But then, just four days later, he'd tasted his first tournament disappointment. Real Madrid had been knocked out of the Copa Del Rey by their bitter rivals, Atlético Madrid.

Then, just three days after that, Jude had got Real back up and firing. He'd scored their crucial first goal against Almeira, while they were trailing 0-2. They'd gone on to win 3-2, which had kept their La Liga title hopes on track.

Then Jude had scored a brace in a 4-0 thrashing of Girona. They were a side who were emerging as a serious title contender, so this bought Jude's team more space at the top of the table.

And most recently, Jude had played in his second El Clásico of the La Liga season. Amazingly, as he'd done in the first tie, Jude had scored a 90th-minute winner to cement Real's position at the top of the table.

In the Champions League, they'd faced Manchester City in the quarter-finals and, once again, Jude had played a significant role. The match had been cagey and at the end of the second leg the score had been 1-1. Neither team had been able to find the back of the net in extra time, so penalties had been needed to decide a winner.

Luka Modrić had missed his penalty, and with City scoring their first penalty but missing their second,

Jude had had the chance to equalise. He'd made no mistake from the spot, drawing Real level and giving his team the momentum to turn it around. They ended up winning 4-3 on penalties, securing their place in the Champions League semi-finals.

Somehow, Jude had even found time to score a stoppage-time equaliser for England in a friendly against Belgium. Jude was in the form of his life.

That brought him back to the game at hand. If Real could beat relegation-threatened Cadiz today, and if Barcelona failed to beat Girona, Real would be crowned La Liga champions.

Jude understood why he'd been benched. The manager, Carlo Ancelotti, wanted to rest his star players for their second leg of the Champions League semi-final against Bayern Munich, in just four days' time. Real had fought hard for a 2-2 draw in the first leg and, with the second leg at home, Jude needed to be fully fit to make the most of it.

The early stages of the game were surprisingly finely balanced, even though Cadiz were defending for their lives against the threat of relegation. The large number of changes that Real Madrid had made from their usual starting line-up was clearly slowing their play down.

As the game progressed, Jude watched in awe from the bench as Luka began to dictate the tempo. Even though the legendary Croatian midfielder was coming to the end of his career, Jude saw that he could still control a match.

At half-time, the score remained 0-0, but just five minutes after the restart, Luka found a pinpoint pass into the feet of Brahim Díaz on the edge of the Cadiz penalty area. Brahim jinked one way and then the other, sending defenders flying, before unleashing a rocket into the top corner of the net.

Real Madrid had the lead – and one hand on the La Liga trophy.

Then, with 25 minutes to go and Real firmly in control, Ancelotti turned to his bench.

"Jude, get on there and see the game out for me," the manager instructed.

Jude didn't need asking twice. He warmed up on the touchline as quickly as he could, before being subbed on for Arda Güler.

It took him only two minutes to make his mark.

Picking the ball up on the edge of the final third, Jude fed the ball into Luka's path. He in turn found Brahim, who sped towards the byline. Looking up, Brahim spotted Jude's perfectly-timed run into the box and found him with a precise pass.

Jude casually stroked the ball into the bottom corner, to give Real a 2-0 lead. It was game over.

Real Madrid saw the rest of the game out with ease, with Joselu adding a third goal late on, to make the final score 3-0.

At full-time, the crowd cheered and applauded the Real Madrid players, who they expected had just made the final step towards La Liga glory. Now all they had to do was wait to see if Barcelona could continue the fight into another week.

Barcelona's match against Girona had kicked off just as Real's was finishing so, after a quick debrief in the dressing room, the Real players had gathered to watch the second half of the Barça game.

At half-time, Barcelona were leading 2-1, meaning that Real would have to fight another day for the title.

But then, in the space of 10 second-half minutes, the game was flipped completely on its head. Girona found three quick-fire goals, to give themselves an astonishing 4-2 lead over Barça.

The Real players watching on TV couldn't quite believe it and, looking at the distraught Barcelona players on the screen, it was clear that they couldn't believe it either.

Shortly afterwards, the referee blew the final whistle. Girona had beaten Barcelona 4-2 and, with that, Real Madrid were La Liga champions.

Jude was a league champion for the first time.

With the Girona versus Barça post-match discussions still playing in the background on the TV, Jude joined his team-mates in their celebrations.

This wasn't the way he'd imagined winning the league – he'd thought they'd be sharing the moment on the pitch, in front of their supporters, but he knew they'd get their chance to celebrate at the Champions League semi-final, in just four days' time.

Jude couldn't believe how successful his first season with the Spanish giants had been. In just that one season, he'd won two trophies – in the Super Cup and La Liga – and he was still in the running for the Champions League.

No matter what happened in the second leg against Bayern, Jude knew that this first taste of significant silverware wouldn't be his last with Real Madrid.

And with Euro 2024 with England on the near horizon, he felt more ready than ever before.

He was Jude Bellingham – and he'd barely started.

HOW MANY HAVE YOU READ?